For Bob and Marjorie, with love

First published in Great Britain 1986
by Methuen Children's Books Ltd
11 New Fetter Lane, London EC4P 4EE
Copyright © 1986 Heather S. Buchanan
Printed in Great Britain

ISBN 0 416 53900 9

Matilda Mouse's Garden

Heather S. Buchanan

Methuen Children's Books

The long cold winter was nearly over and the deep snow was beginning to melt away. Matilda Mouse looked out of the window and saw that Spring was coming at last.

Matilda lived in a cottage kitchen with her mother and father and twin baby brothers. Their house was an old teapot which sat unused on the mantelpiece, and their door was a hole at the side where three cracks met. The lid of the teapot was lost, so they could climb in and out of the top too.

The mouse family were safe in their tea-pot, well hidden from the old lady who lived in the cottage, and her cat Harriet. At night they lit old candle stubs that their father found and dragged home. They slept in empty matchboxes hanging on pieces of knitting wool from a pencil wedged across the inside of the teapot, and they collected useful odds and ends from the kitchen at night whenever they could.

Oliver and Humphrey, Matilda's twin baby brothers, grew naughtier and naughtier as they got bigger. Matilda was supposed to look after them while her parents were out looking for food at night, but sometimes they squeezed out of the teapot through the little hole at the side and scampered away to play. Poor Matilda worried terribly until she found them again in the kitchen.

One night, Oliver and Humphrey squeezed themselves through the gap at the bottom of the kitchen door, and escaped into the garden. Luckily, Matilda saw them go, and ran after them as fast as she could. She got stuck under the door and tore her dress, but at last she managed to squeeze through too.

What a wonderful sight she saw! There
were twigs all twinkling with frost,
beautiful white leaves, an old snow-
covered log, and best of all, white flowers
called snowdrops with green stems and
leaves. Matilda forgot all about chasing
the twins. She just stood spellbound,
gazing up at one of the snowdrops, gently
touching it with her paw.

Suddenly Matilda remembered the danger the twins were in. If the cat caught them she would swallow them in one mouthful. There they were, behind the log, throwing snowballs! Matilda called them, smacked them and took them home. Once inside the cottage she wiped their wet paws on her skirt so that they would not leave mouse marks on the floor for the old lady to find in the morning.

Next day Matilda peeped out of the teapot
and saw the old lady bring out some
packets of flower seeds. She planted them
in soil in wooden boxes, and then she put
them on the window ledge to catch the
spring sunshine. Matilda watched,
delighted, as one of the packets of seeds
fell onto the floor. She longed to grow her
own flowers in the garden, like the
snowdrops.

That night she waited until Humphrey and Oliver were asleep and then she set off to fetch the seed packet. Getting it home was quite a struggle. She had to roll it up to carry it. But when it was safely inside the teapot she counted out twelve seeds, and stood the packet with the picture of Cornflowers on it beside her bed. Then she curled up in her matchbox and sighed with happiness.

A few weeks later, when the moon was
out, Matilda crept out to plant her seeds.
She watched carefully for Harriet, but

everything seemed quiet. She was sad to
see that the snowdrops had gone, but she
made twelve little holes with a twig near
the place where she had seen them
growing. Very gently, she pushed a seed
deep down into each hole, and sprinkled
some soil over it to keep it warm. Then
she turned to go home.

But just as she turned she sensed with her whiskers that something was wrong. She sniffed hard. She could smell Harriet the cat. She froze.

There was a big waterbutt nearby. Matilda pressed herself in behind it – but then drew back, horrified. Hiding there too was someone with frightening red eyes. She wanted to run away, but she had to stay still, because if she moved or squeaked, the cat would see her. She was absolutely terrified.

After a while when Matilda dared to look more carefully behind the waterbutt, she saw that the eyes only belonged to an old toad. He had watched her plant her seeds, and would never have hurt her. He even said he would frighten the slugs away for her.

At last Harriet went on her way. Matilda thanked the toad and scampered home. Back in her matchbox bed she dreamed about her seeds. She longed to creep out to see if they were growing, but somehow she knew they were not ready for her.

One day when the sun was high in the sky Matilda felt the right time had come. She took a great risk, and crept outside to see if her flowers had grown.

They were lovely! Deep blue and very tall. Matilda nibbled through a stalk, and very carefully she carried one flower back to the cottage. She put it in the milkjug on the kitchen table, to say thank you to the old lady for the seeds. The old lady never could guess how the flower came to be there, and Matilda smiled to herself as she watched from behind the teapot!